AN UNOFFICIA

DIARY OF A

ROBLOX

PRO

OBBY CHALLENGE

By Ari Avatar

SCHOLASTIC INC.

If you purchased this book without a cover, you should be aware that this book is stolen property. It was reported as "unsold and destroyed" to the publisher, and neither the author nor the publisher has received any payment for this "stripped book."

© 2022 Scholastic Australia

First published by Scholastic Australia Pty Limited in 2022.

All rights reserved. Published by Scholastic Inc., *Publishers since 1920*. SCHOLASTIC and associated logos are trademarks and/or registered trademarks of Scholastic Inc.

The publisher does not have any control over and does not assume any responsibility for author or third-party websites or their content.

No part of this publication may be reproduced, stored in a retrieval system, or transmitted in any form or by any means, electronic, mechanical, photocopying, recording, or otherwise, without written permission of the publisher. For information regarding permission, write to Scholastic Inc., Attention: Permissions Department, 557 Broadway, New York, NY 10012.

This book is a work of fiction. Names, characters, places, and incidents are either the product of the author's imagination or are used fictitiously, and any resemblance to actual persons, living or dead, business establishments, events, or locales is entirely coincidental.

ISBN 978-1-338-86348-2

10 9 8 7 6 5 4 3 2   23 24 25 26 27

Printed in the U.S.A.   37

This edition first printing, June 2023

Cover design by Hannah Janzen and Ashley Vargas

Internal design by Paul Hallam

Typeset in Dawet Ayu, Silkscreen, LOGX-10, Apercu Mono, and Ate Bit

The paper in this book is FSC® certified. FSC® promotes environmentally responsible, socially beneficial, and economically viable management of the world's forests.

MONDAY AFTERNOON

"Watch this," I said, throwing a popcorn piece into the air and catching it in my mouth.

"Watch *this*!" Jez said, copying me, but before the popcorn could land in her mouth, a long, hairy arm reached out and snatched it.

"Dash!" she yelled.

Zeke's **DREAM PET,** a sloth, smiled sleepily as he chewed the stolen morsel.

"That's the **FASTEST** I've ever seen him move." Zeke laughed.

Dash climbed onto Zeke's bed and grabbed the rope that was strung across the ceiling. He climbed slowly, hand over hand, until he got to the far end of Zeke's bedroom. Then he pulled himself onto the top of the dresser, where he had a little nest of cushions waiting for him.

Zeke's bedroom is the **COOLEST.** It is huge—like, three times the size of mine—and basically his dad had made it into an **OBBY COURSE.** There are ropes hanging from the ceiling, gymnastics rings, a chin-up bar, and even a rock-climbing wall opposite his bed. It totally helped that his dad is a real-life obby designer. He works for the army and creates obby courses for them to train on.

"Hey, Ari, watch THIS!" Zeke said, jumping up from his bed where he was sitting. He threw a piece of popcorn high into the air and it traveled across his bedroom.

I smirked—it was a dud throw and there was **NO WAY** he could catch that!

But suddenly, Zeke did a backflip and then he ran fast toward the popcorn as it started its descent. Then he ran up the wall. Literally. Like, his feet pounded its surface, leaving light smudges, then he pushed hard off it and curled his body into a **SOMERSAULT.**

As he landed, he looked up, opened his mouth, and the popcorn piece fell onto his tongue with a soft "plop!"

"WHOA!" Jez gasped.

"Epic!" I said, high-fiving him.

Zeke has been my best friend since we were tiny avatars. And he has always been a **PARKOUR PRO.** I won't lie—I'm always just a teensy bit jealous of his sick skills. But when I looked around his bedroom, it was pretty obvious why. I mean, all I had at home was one boring old chin-up bar in the garage.

"OK, I may not be an **OBBY PRO** in real life, but I'm totally an obby pro online!" Jez said, whipping open her laptop.

Zeke and I leaned in to see her

latest creation. Jez is the biggest **TECH PRO** and can code just about anything. She likes to create obbys online and show them to Zeke's dad. Once, he even used some of her designs in one of his real obbys.

The screen lit up as Jez typed her login.

"WOW!" Zeke breathed.

Jez's obby design looked amazing.

"Watch this," she said.

Her avatar leaped across the screen, bounding from block to block. Then the screen lit up with orange as a firepit **BLAZED** under her obby course.

"You've gotta time your jump so you don't get fried," she said, pointing to the firepit below her avatar. "But you also have to watch out for—"

Before she could finish, a massive, **SPINNING SAW** dropped down from above, chopping her avatar in half.

"Whoops!" she said as the game ended. "I need to work on that. Is your dad home, Zeke? I want to show him how much I've done on my obby."

"He's working on the army base today, sorry," Zeke said. "I'm sure he'll check it out next time."

Jez nodded and shut her laptop.

"So, what do you wanna do?" I asked. "Should we go outside and time ourselves on the prototype obby you have in your backyard?"

Zeke shook his head. "Dad took it down."

"Why?" Jez asked.

"He's starting a new one. It's going to be **AWESOME.** Come over in a couple of days when it's all set up," Zeke said. "I've seen part of the design and it's so cool. But he's still tweaking it. I think he'd like to see some of your ideas, Jez!"

Jez's eyes lit up.

I glanced at the clock on Zeke's wall. "Oh man," I said. "I've gotta go!

I was meant to be helping Mom this afternoon."

I jumped up and high-fived Zeke and fist-bumped Jez. "See you avatars tomorrow at school."

As I walked to the door, I turned and saw Zeke doing some cool tricks on his rings. I was definitely going to practice my obby skills before his dad showed us the new prototype obby. I wanted to **SMASH IT!**

TUESDAY LUNCHTIME

I sat down at the lunch table with Zeke and Jez, and started munching my sandwich.

NOM, NOM, NOM.

"So, guess what happened after you left Zeke's house yesterday?" Jez said to me.

"What?"

"Zeke's dad came home and

I showed him my online obby. He said it was **SICK!"** Jez beamed.

"He actually said *sick?*" I asked, disbelievingly.

"OK, no, he said some kind of old-avatar word like 'superb,' but he totally meant *sick*!" Jez laughed.

"Dad is going to use part of Jez's design in his latest obby for the army," Zeke said proudly.

"WHOA! Which part?" I asked.

"The part with the firepit!" Jez said.

The firepit was where Jez's avatar was, like, six meters in the air, and there were flames **BLASTING** up underneath her while a circular saw dropped from above.

"Really? Isn't that, like, totally **DEADLY?**" I said.

"The prototype at home won't actually be deadly," Zeke laughed. "But they need the hardest, deadliest obbys to train the army for life-and-death situations."

I frowned.

"Don't worry," Zeke said, sensing my concern. "The soldiers training will have protective suits on. They won't really be sawn in half or **BURNED** to a crisp!"

I relaxed. "Cool."

"Dad is setting it up over the next few days, but the tame version should be ready for us to try by Friday. Wanna come over and test it?" Zeke asked.

"YES!" Jez and I said in unison.

"Test what?" a voice jeered.

Trip. **UGH.**

Trip is the most arrogant avatar on earth. His mom is the mayor of our town, and he is the **BIGGEST BULLY** in the whole school.

"Just Zeke's dad's epic new obby," Jez said with her eyebrows raised.

"I bet I could do it," Trip taunted.

"As if!" Zeke said.

Trip did a **BOX-JUMP** onto our table without even using his

hands. If I didn't dislike him
so much, I'd probably have said
it was cool.

"Get off," Jez said, moving her
lunch away from his dirty shoes.

Trip did a **BACKWARD**
SOMERSAULT off the

table and landed with a thud on the ground.

"Zeke can do that, **EZ!**" Jez said.

"Go on, then," Trip challenged.

Zeke stood up on the table and effortlessly did a backward somersault onto the ground. It was **HIGHER** and cooler than Trip's, and other avatars looked up from their lunches, impressed.

Trip scowled. "What about *this?*" he said, jumping onto the table again. He ran across the rectangular surface and did a side-sault before landing on top of the empty table next to us.

"Cool!" a couple of younger avatars said.

Trip beamed.

Zeke raised his eyebrows, then ran and did a somersault with a **HALF TWIST,** landing on the other table.

"EPIC!" another kid yelled.

Trip growled, then took a run-up

and **VAULTED** over the garbage, landing on the other side.

Zeke did the same.

A crowd had gathered around Zeke and Trip, watching the **PARKOUR CHALLENGE.**

"What about *this*?" Trip said.

He ran up to the balcony railing that looked over the playground area below, and launched himself over it. The crowd **GASPED** as everyone looked over the edge to see if Trip was OK. It was only

a short drop down, and I knew
Zeke could do it **EASILY.**

Before Zeke moved, Trip jumped
and grabbed the balcony railing
above him, hauling himself back up
to the level Zeke was on. Some of
the kids applauded.

"Your move," he taunted.

Zeke shook his head, knowing the
challenge was too easy. But as he
launched himself toward the railing,
I saw Trip tap the bottom of Zeke's
foot, sending him off balance.
Zeke **HURTLED** over the

balcony to the level below, landing
with a **CRASH** onto the grass.

Some avatars started laughing.

"Are you OK?!" Jez yelled.

"Yeah," Zeke said, standing up
and dusting himself off.

Trip cackled and walked away.

Zeke came back to our table and sat down with a huff.

"He's so annoying," Jez mumbled. "He thinks he's such a **PRO** at everything."

"He's got nothing on you, bruh," I said to Zeke. "You'd **SMASH HIM** in an obby any day."

Zeke smiled. "Well, he's not invited to my place to try the obby!" he said. "So who cares?"

I nodded in agreement. None of us wanted Trip around.

WEDNESDAY NIGHT

I walked downstairs and **PLONKED** myself in a chair at the dining table.

"Drinks, please, Ari," Dad said.

I got back up, dragging my feet behind me, as I grabbed the glasses and water jug.

We all sat and started eating our tacos.

NOM, NOM, NOM.

"Anything **EXCITING** happen today?" Mom asked.

"We got our block-building assignment back and I got the top grade in the class!" Ally sang.

"Go, Ally!" Dad cheered.

"Great job!" Mom praised. "And what about you, Ari?" Mom asked.

"Nah, nothing today. But, Zeke's dad has this awesome new obby, and Jez and I are invited on

Friday to try it out!" I said as
I took a big bite of my taco.

"Only if all your chores are done,"
Mom warned.

I **ROLLED** my eyes. Dad gave
me a serious look.

"Yeah, of course," I said, irritated.
"But can I go?"

Mom nodded and I fist-pumped
the air.

I finished eating, then ran upstairs
to check if Zeke had messaged me.

Zeke: Ari, are you there?

. . .

Ari: I'm here! Wassup?

Zeke: Dad has pretty much finished the prototype. Come over Friday?

Ari: Yessss! Mom said it's OK.

Zeke: Sick! GTG.

Ari: C u l8r, bruh.

FRIDAY AFTERNOON

I arrived at Zeke's house after school. I didn't even knock on the front door—I've known Zeke's family for most of my life and they always say their house is open to me at any time. I entered and called out, "I'm here!" and Zeke appeared at the top of the stairs. He jumped onto the banister and **SLID** down, landing neatly on his feet at the bottom.

"Jez here yet?" I asked.

Zeke shook his head and beckoned me to follow him through to the kitchen.

"Hi, Ari, how's it going?" Zeke's dad asked, looking up from his laptop at the dining table.

"Good, thanks. Can't wait to try your **NEW OBBY**," I answered.

"It's a beauty!" Zeke's dad said. "And I've used some of Jez's ideas too. Oh, here she is now!"

Jez walked through the door and fist-bumped both me and Zeke.

Then she walked over to Zeke's dad and gave him a high five.

"Can't wait to see how it all turned out," she said, craning her head to see some of the obby through the back window.

Zeke's dad smiled and waved for us to follow him to the back door. We walked through it and into the yard.

"Cool!" Jez and I breathed together.

The obby was the **BIGGEST**

prototype I'd ever seen. It was made of unpainted wood, big plastic blocks, and rough ropes. I knew the real obby would look much cleaner and fancier than this one. This was just a practice build.

Zeke's dad walked us through the obby, pointing out all the different parts.

"So, you start down here," he said. "You have to climb this pipe and get to the platform. Jump from block to block, but **DON'T FALL!** See the red material under the blocks?"

We all nodded.

"That represents the **LAVA** that's in the real thing. When you pass that part, you climb up this ladder, even higher. The next set of floating blocks are moving, so you have to time your jump or you'll fall into the lava. Once you are across that, you go down the slide, back toward the bottom level. Along here, you enter this metal **TUNNEL.**"

We all peered into a dark pipe that had a **BIG BOULDER** rolling up and down inside.

"How do you get through the pipe with that boulder? It would squish you!" Zeke said.

"Well, this boulder wouldn't— it's fake. But in the real obby, you have to jump into the little holes in the pipe while it passes. You have to time it right too. There are holes the whole way up the pipe to protect you, but you have to watch the boulder so you can safely **HIDE** in a hole before it rolls over you."

We walked past the pipe to another ladder.

"Climb this ladder and then walk along the thin metal paths. They're pretty narrow, so you have to be careful," he said.

"Lava below?" I asked.

He shook his head. "No, this time it's **LASER PADS.** You fall on them and you're fried! Once you're through that part, you get to the **FINAL** challenge. This is based on Jez's obby," Zeke's dad said.

Jez beamed proudly.

"You have to navigate these spinning blocks, jumping from one to the next. But underneath is a firepit, which sometimes shoots flames up underneath you. And pay attention to what's above, because these lasers shoot downward—just like Jez's circular saws."

"But this one is just a prototype, right?" I clarified.

Zeke's dad laughed. "Yes, Ari, you're perfectly safe. The lasers are just lights. And I've got padding on the ground in case you fall."

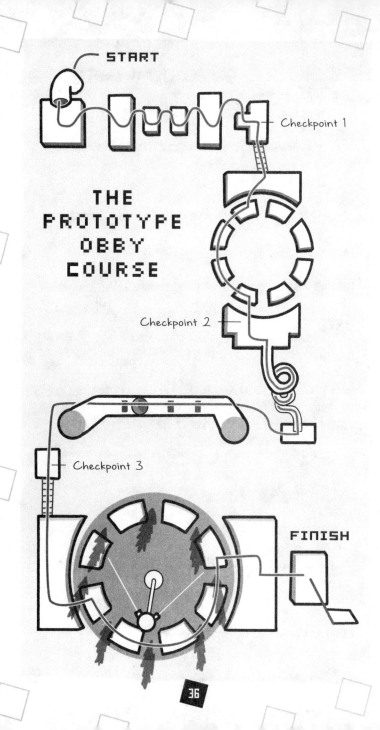

START

Checkpoint 1

THE
PROTOTYPE
OBBY
COURSE

Checkpoint 2

Checkpoint 3

FINISH

I breathed a sigh of relief.

"OK, Zeke, why don't you go first to show your friends how it works, since you've had a turn before?"

Zeke nodded and leaped into action. He **SHIMMIED** up the pipe and stood on the platform, staring out at the floating blocks. He carefully jumped from block to block.

"Watch out for the lava below!" Jez joked.

Zeke climbed the next ladder, and

we had to put our hands up by
our eyes to shield out the sun.
He was **SO HIGH!**

Zeke was just about to start
jumping onto the next row of
floating blocks when his dad
called out, "Wait there a second!
I think you forgot something!"

He pulled a lever at the bottom of the obby and the floating blocks started to move around in a circle.

"Aw man!" Zeke groaned.

I could see the concentration on his face as he counted the blocks that **WHIZZED** by. Then he leaped into the air and landed on one of them with a thud. He almost lost his balance as the block moved, but quickly found his footing.

He jumped from the moving block to the next platform.

"That's the second checkpoint!"
his dad called.

Next, Zeke plonked onto his back
and **ZOOMED** down the steep,
slippery slide, which sent him
hurtling toward the lower level.
He jumped up when he got to the
bottom and peered into the pipe.

On his hands and knees, Zeke
shimmied in. We could see into the
dark pipe and we heard the low
rumbling of the **BOULDER**
as it made its way toward him.
He scurried through the pipe to
the first hole and slipped inside,

crouching down in a tiny ball. The boulder glided over the hole where Zeke was safely hidden. He jumped out of the hole and crawled as fast as he could toward the next one.

"QUICK, ZEKE! The boulder is almost back!" I yelled.

With only a millisecond to spare, Zeke slipped into the next hole, keeping himself safe from the passing boulder. Even though Zeke's dad said the boulder was fake and it wouldn't hurt us, I couldn't help the anxious feeling in my stomach as the rock **CHASED** my best friend.

Zeke made it through the pipe just before the boulder touched him.

"You're **A PRO!**" Jez whooped.

"Checkpoint!" Zeke's dad yelled. "Phase two passed!"

Zeke climbed the last ladder and got himself ready for the final part of the obby—the one based on Jez's design.

"These flames are fast!" he said.

Shooting up from below were red lights, which, although harmless, were meant to represent the **FLAME BLASTS.** Then from above, blue lasers shot down.

"How do you time this right?" I asked Jez. "It's, like, whenever a flame stops, a laser starts."

"There's a rhythm to it," she said mischievously.

Zeke hesitated. It was the first time in the whole course where he looked uncomfortable.

"Come on, Zeke," his dad
encouraged.

Zeke mumbled to himself and then
took a flying leap. He landed on
the first block just as a flame of
red shot up, narrowly missing him.
He **SOARED** to the next block,
watching carefully for the coming
flame. But he wasn't taking notice
of what was above. A blue laser
shot down, connecting with Zeke.
A loud buzzer went off, indicating
that Zeke had **FAILED.**

"Not again!" he moaned. He slipped
down the rope at the end of the

obby. "I still haven't conquered that last phase," he said, annoyed. "Why'd you make it so *hard*, Jez?"

Jez grinned. She liked that her invention was difficult.

Zeke's dad high-fived Jez. "It's such a challenging phase, isn't it? Jez did a great job. This is exactly what we need when training the army avatars. You never know what kind of danger they'll find themselves in, so we need to **CHALLENGE** them as much as we can."

"Ari, you up?" Zeke asked me as he took a big swig of water from his bottle.

"**GAME ON!**" I said, excited to have my turn.

I climbed the pole to the first obstacle, the floating blocks. I **JUMPED** from one to the next, landing in a crouched position so I could keep my balance.

I breathed out deeply.

"Phase one complete!" Zeke's dad declared.

I climbed to the next level, which had the moving blocks. They seemed to be going so much faster from up here.

I hesitated, feeling unsure of myself.

"YOU CAN DO IT, ARI!" Zeke encouraged.

I went to jump and totally mistimed it. The block sailed by and I **PLUMMETED** down to the "lava," which was just a big, thick red mat.

OOF!

"Aw man! I failed!" I exclaimed, frustrated.

"Have another go," Zeke's dad encouraged me.

"But I'm toast! I'm lava meat. I'm dead!" I said.

Zeke's dad laughed. "It's just for fun, Ari. **TRY AGAIN.**"

I climbed back up to the checkpoint and readied myself to conquer the moving blocks once more.

"The trick is to jump early," Zeke said.

I saw a block approaching.

"NOW!" Zeke yelled.

I hesitated for half a second—
it felt like I was jumping way too
early. But my instincts trusted
Zeke and I jumped anyway. I landed
on the moving block with a thud.

"YEAH! PRO!" Zeke hooted.

The moving block whizzed around
to the next platform and I jumped
off to the following checkpoint.

From there, I **WHOOSHED** down

the slide and landed below. Next was the pipeline.

I crawled inside. It felt darker and squishier than it looked from the outside. I crawled along on my hands and knees until I heard a light **RUMBLING.**

The boulder was approaching! Even though I knew it was fake, it still made my heart beat fast. I crawled as **QUICKLY** as I could and ducked into the first hole. Pulling my head down into my knees, I waited for the rumble of the boulder to pass over. Once

I was sure it was gone, I popped my head up like a meerkat.

I leaped up and started speed-crawling like an avatar baby. That's when I heard the light rumble of the boulder again.

Only a few more steps to get to the next hole! I crawled faster.

"Go, Ari!" Jez yelled.

I dived for the hole, but as I sank into it, I felt the light brush of the fake boulder over my feet. A buzzer went off.

OOF! Failed again.

"I think I got **SQUISHED** by the boulder." I peeked out of the pipeline, embarrassed.

"Ah, barely." Zeke's dad gave me a wink. "I'll allow it."

I smiled and climbed the ladder for the last phase: Jez's fire-and-laser blocks.

I watched as the fire and blue lasers **BLASTED** from above and below. There was no time in between them to get across.

"Jez, is this even possible?"
I moaned.

I could see her mischievous grin.

I jumped onto the first block,
narrowly avoiding a stream of red
flame. Then jumped to the next.
I remembered the laser from above
that had blasted Zeke, so I quickly
ducked out of the way when it
shot down. But before I had the
chance to celebrate, a red fire
laser collided with me.

OOF. Failed again.

BZZZZZZ!

I slid down the rope toward
my friends.

"Well, that was an epic fail."
I laughed. "But it was **SUPER
FUN.**"

Zeke's dad gave me a high five.

Jez had her turn and did a pretty good job. She passed phases one and two, but then got hit by the boulder. And when she got to her final obby, I was sure she'd nail it, since she invented it and all. But to our surprise, she fell off and didn't make it through.

"Sheesh, Jez," Zeke said as he helped her off the mat. "You made an obby that is **SO HARD,** even *you* can't do it!"

"Well, there's a **SECRET** to

that last one that I wasn't ready to show you just yet," she said mischievously.

Zeke's dad winked at her. "Good job, avatars," he said.

"You mean we all got totally **FRIED!**" Zeke laughed.

"Well, yes," Zeke's dad chuckled. "I for one wouldn't ever want to be on this obby course in real life! That would be . . . **DEADLY!**"

SATURDAY AFTERNOON

Zeke: Guess what, bruh?

Ari: Wat?

Zeke: Dad and his crew have been building the obby at the army base. IRL!

Ari: EPIC!

Zeke: And guess what else?

Ari: Wat?

Zeke: He said you, Jez, and I can go with him to the army base to see it IRL!

Ari: AWESOME!

Zeke: He's doing some kind of tour thing for important officials or something in a couple of weeks. But he said we can come.

Ari: Do we get a go on it?

Zeke: LOL, no, bruh! Remember the fire and the lasers? On this obby, they are REAL.

Ari: Oh yeah, 4got that part!

Zeke: Even if we wore the death-proof suits the army avatars wear, I still wouldn't do it.

Ari: It will be cool just to see it tho.

Zeke: GTG. C u @ school.

Ari: L8r, bruh.

59

SATURDAY MORNING, TWO WEEKS LATER

I arrived at Zeke's house and saw Jez was already there.

"Ready to go, team?" Zeke's dad said, ushering us over to the car. "It's a **BIG DAY** and I don't want to be late. There are high-ranking officials from the army, plus some government officials and their families."

"Like, the president?!" I said.

Zeke's dad laughed. "No, not the president. But **THE MAYOR** and her son will be there."

We all stopped dead in our tracks. The mayor of Blockville was . . . Trip's mom! Which meant . . .

NOOOOOOOO!

TRIP was going to be there!

"That's one way to ruin the day," Zeke moaned.

"Oh, it'll be fine," his dad said. "You'll be having way too much fun to be worrying about other avatars there."

Maybe he was right. I hoped so.

SATURDAY, MID-MORNING

We finally pulled into the army base after going through what felt like a hundred checkpoints. Zeke's dad had to scan through lots of security gates and get clearance from the guards. We drove up a long, winding road until we reached a **MASSIVE** metal warehouse.

We got out of the car and joined a small group gathered in front.

"We need to wait for the other officials to arrive before we start the tour," Zeke's dad whispered.

More cars pulled up. Official-looking avatars stepped out, some in uniforms and some in nice suits. A **FANCY CAR** arrived last, and the driver opened the front passenger door for a tall woman. She wore big sunglasses and bright lipstick. The driver then opened the back passenger door for another avatar. The newspaper reporter who was there hurried over and took a photo of the pair.

"Hello, adoring fans!" the boy avatar said.

"Trip's arrived." Zeke rolled his eyes.

Trip beamed like he was a little prince arriving with the queen.

"Welcome, Madame Mayor, and welcome, Trip," Zeke's dad said, shaking hands with Trip's mom. "I can't wait to show you what we've been developing here for army training. It's really exciting."

"Will I get a go on the obby?" Trip asked.

Zeke's dad gave a chuckle,
but Trip remained stone-faced.

"Oh," said Zeke's dad. "Sorry,
buddy, I can't let any young
avatar on there. It's way too
DANGEROUS."

"Don't worry, Trippy," the mayor
said. "I'll buy you a big ice-cream
sundae on the way home instead."

Trip sulked.

"Why don't you go join your
friends over there?" the mayor
said, pointing in our direction.

Jez made a quiet gagging sound.

"I guess I'm stuck with you **LOSERS** for the day," Trip said after he walked over to us. "It's a shame we can't do the obby—I'd **SMASH** you all just like I did to Zeke at school."

"You only beat him because you **CHEATED,"** Jez said.

"Yeah, right," Trip taunted. "More like Zeke is just hopeless at obbys."

"Everyone, if you'd like to follow me, please," Zeke's dad said, starting the tour. He scanned his pass and a big metal roller door slowly opened.

In the first room, we looked at all the different parts that made up the obbys in the warehouse. There were cool laser blocks, ropes, pipes, electronics, and a big vat of hot liquid with a **POISON** sign on it.

"Don't touch that one!" Zeke's dad said with a wink.

"This is **BORING**," Trip whined. "When do we see the obby?"

"Keep up with the group, everyone!" Zeke's dad said. "If you fall behind, you'll get locked in and won't have a scan card to get out."

We followed Zeke's dad to the next door.

"Through here is the obby you're all waiting to see," Zeke's dad said dramatically.

"At last," mumbled Trip.

We entered the room and it opened out into a massive, cavernous space. Our mouths fell open.

"WHOA!" we all breathed.

This obby was even cooler than the prototype. It had shining walls, glowing blocks, and bright, bubbling lava. I could feel its heat as we got closer.

"Stay back, everyone," Zeke's dad said, holding up his hands.

At that moment, some **ARMY AVATARS** arrived. They were wearing what looked like space suits and helmets.

"These suits are state-of-the-art

designs," Zeke's dad explained. "They protect the avatar from any of the **LASERS** or **LAVA.** Without them, you'd be risking your life going into the obby."

Zeke's dad patted an avatar on the back. "Now, this avatar here is going to show us how it's done."

The avatar climbed to the first platform. He approached the floating bricks and jumped from block to block.

We watched carefully as the avatar went through the next phases of the obby. It was pretty similar to the prototype we'd done. As he cleared each obstacle, a loud voice would say, *"Checkpoint cleared."*

He finally made it to the last obstacle—it was Jez's design with the flames **SHOOTING** up from the lava below and lasers shooting down from above.

The avatar **DODGED** the first flame and ducked the first laser. Then he leaped to the next brick.

But as he avoided the next flame, the laser shot him in the back. A bright light zapped through the air as it hit him, and he **CRASHED** down below.

We all gasped.

But then he emerged from the steaming lava and some other army avatars hosed him off to decontaminate him.

"Now, I don't need to remind you, if this avatar didn't have his suit on, he'd be a blocky hot milkshake right now!" Zeke's dad said.

I looked at the **OOZING** lava and the shimmering lasers above and swallowed hard.

It was **TERRIFYING.**

SATURDAY, A BIT LATER . . .

Everyone began wandering around the obby, pointing out all the exciting parts.

"Man, I wish I could have a go on that thing," Trip said.

"You wouldn't last a second."
I laughed.

"Oh yeah?"

"Yeah!"

"Come on, everyone. To the next room!" Zeke's dad announced.

We started to follow the others, but I felt something pulling me back.

"I **DARE** you to climb up the first pipe," Trip whispered.

"C'mon, Ari!" Zeke yelled, catching up to his dad.

Before I could respond, Trip taunted, "Are you **CHICKEN?**"

"Trip, I'm not going on the obby,"
I told him. "It's a **DEATH
TRAP.** We don't have
protective suits."

Trip grabbed my arm. "I bet you
that I could do the first part. It
isn't even that dangerous—there's
no lava on phase one."

"Come on, you avatars!" Jez yelled.

Trip ran over to the obby and
touched the pipe that you had
to climb up to start.

"Trip," I hissed. "Get back!"

I looked at Zeke disappearing through the doors with his dad. We had to get out of there before we were **LEFT BEHIND.**

I rolled my eyes.

"Trip, NOW," I said, running over to him.

"Ari!" Jez jogged toward me. "We have to stay with the group!"

"Trip's climbing the obby!" I said. "We need to get Zeke's dad."

Jez nodded and we turned to

run back to Zeke's dad when we
heard a big . . .

WHOOOOSH!

The door slammed shut and
a locking mechanism clunked
into place.

"Good one, Trip, now we're
LOCKED in here!" I shouted.

The lights all turned off with a click. The only light visible was the glow of the **LAVA** and the blocks on the obby. I shivered.

"They'll be back—my mom will notice I'm not there," Trip's voice called out from the other side of the room.

Jez and I carefully walked through the darkness, back to the **GLOWING** obby. Trip was almost at the top of the pipe.

"Trip, get down now," Jez called.

"I just want to get to the platform," he said.

"If you try the obby, you'll be **FRIED!**" I said.

"I just want to try the first phase," Trip insisted.

Trip got to the top of the platform. He looked at the quivering blocks that made up phase one. He did a **SOARING JUMP** and then landed on the first block.

"Nailed it!" he hollered.

"Trip, that's enough. Come down and we can try to get some help to get out of here," Jez said.

He jumped to the next block, landing heavily. The block **GLOWED** white under his feet.

Jez looked at me, concerned.

Trip did another three jumps and safely landed on the platform on the other side.

"Checkpoint one cleared," the electronic voice said over the speaker.

Trip jumped up and down. "I'm an obby pro! I'm an obby **PRO!**"

"OK, you've had your fun. Now let's GO," Jez said.

"I'll get down once Ari has a turn," Trip said.

"What?! No!" I yelled.

"Well, your **BLOCKHEAD** friend Zeke isn't in here and I already bloxxed him at school. I bet you can't do phase one!" Trip laughed.

I looked at the obby. Phase one was the same as what I did at Zeke's house. It wasn't very hard and there wasn't really any risk. No lasers. No flames. No lava.

"You don't have to, Ari," Jez said.

"I know. But I may as well while we're stuck in here!" I said with a smile.

"Just promise you won't go farther than **PHASE ONE**," she said in an uncertain voice.

I nodded and climbed up the pipe.

The top of the platform was
a lot **HIGHER** than the one
at Zeke's house. I swallowed hard.

The white blocks quivered in
the air. I took a flying leap and
landed on the first one.

OOF!

Then I jumped to the second.
Then the third. I hopped from
block to block until I was on the
other side with Trip.

"Checkpoint one cleared," an
electronic voice boomed.

"There. See? Told you I could do it." I smirked. "Zeke isn't the only obby pro."

"Whatever. Let's get out of here," Trip said as he turned to jump back to the first block. But he couldn't move.

"Hey, what the . . . ?" He pushed his body forward, but it was like he was banging into an **INVISIBLE** glass wall.

"Stop messing around and jump back," I said, annoyed.

He held up his hands and tried
to extend them forward. But they
hit the invisible wall again.

"Wh—what is this?" he stammered.

I pushed Trip to the side
and held out my arms. They
COLLIDED with a cold glass
wall, which was definitely not
there a moment ago.

"Jez!" I called. "What's happening?!"

Jez skipped over to the computer
and started typing something
into the system. "Oh, great!" She
sounded panicked. **"YOU CAN'T
GO BACKWARD."**

"What do you mean?!" Trip and
I yelled in unison.

"The course is designed so that once you start, you have to keep going. Each checkpoint creates an invisible **BARRIER** that stops the avatar from going backward."

"But . . . but I can't do the course!" Trip screamed, looking ahead to the lava.

"Jez, can you, like, disarm the system?" I asked.

"I can't!" she said. "This program is based on a type of code that's very hard to hack. It would take me days to crack it."

"We'll wait, then," I said, looking nervously at Trip. "Someone will come and save us soon."

"Uh, Ari." Jez's voice shook as she looked up from the computer screen.

I could just make out what was on the screen from where I was on the platform. A **TIMER** was counting down.

15:02

15:01

15:00

"What is it?" Trip said.

"Um, bruh. There's a countdown on this obby," Jez said.

"And what happens if it gets to zero?" Trip asked quietly.

Jez pulled up some more boxes on the screen. Then she looked at me, and even in the darkness I could see that her block face was pale. "You'll fail the course. And it will . . . laser-blast you."

"LASER-BLAST US?!"
Trip and I screamed.

"There's only one choice," Jez said. "Unless someone comes in the next fourteen minutes, you need to finish the course."

"I CAN'T!" Trip wailed. "GET MY MOMMY!"

"What are we gonna do?!" I said. There was no way we could do the course. We'd be blasted to

SMITHEREENS.

"Jez, can you do anything on the system?!" I asked, thinking fast.

"I can help you both," she yelled. "I can look at how each obstacle is set up and tell you how to get past it. It's your only shot."

"WE HAVE TO TRY," I told Trip. "I think we can do it. You're an obby pro, right?"

"Phase two," Jez said. "Climb the ladder to the next platform."

"Come on, Trip. Up the ladder. One step at a time," I urged.

I climbed the ladder and perched on the next platform. Then I turned to make sure Trip was following. He joined me at the top and we looked out at the next phase, where the blocks were zooming by. I remembered from the prototype that the blocks moved fast and the trick Zeke taught me.

"I can't do it!" Trip wailed.

"I've done this before!" I told him. "You have to wait, then jump a little bit early, just before the block arrives. Watch." I pointed to the next block coming toward me. "Here's the rhythm: Wait . . . GO! Wait . . . GO!" I didn't actually jump, but just pointed to where the block **WHIZZED** past.

Trip sniveled.

"Do you want me to go first?" I offered.

Trip nodded.

I looked down and underneath us was a bubbling pool of **HOT,**

RED LAVA. I had to get this right.

In my head, I repeated the pattern.

Wait. Go. Wait. Go.

Then I summoned all my bravery.

WAIT . . . **GO!**

I leaped into the air and landed on
the whooshing block with a thud.

"Yeah, Ari!" Jez cheered.

"Checkpoint two cleared."

The block zoomed around the
circle, and as I saw the platform
approaching on the other side,
I leaped into the air again and
landed on the platform with a thud.

"Your turn, Trip!"

Trip's legs were **SHAKING.**

"Wait and . . ." I instructed. **"GO!"**

Trip soared through the air and landed on the edge of the block. He wobbled, then regained his balance. As he whizzed around, I held out my arms and beckoned him to jump for the platform. He landed on me with a bang.

"Checkpoint two cleared."

"I don't want to hurry you too much, but you've only got **TEN MINUTES,"** Jez yelled.

SATURDAY, TEN MINUTES TO GO . . .

Just like Zeke's backyard obby, there was a slide taking us to the bottom of the obby. We slid down it as fast as we could, remembering that time was not on our side.

This took us to **PHASE THREE:** the pipe and boulder.

"Trip, this pipe will have little holes in it. You need to crawl along it

SUPER FAST and then duck into a hole as soon as you find it. Crouch into a ball until the boulder passes over," I explained.

"The boulder?!" Trip said.

At that exact moment, we heard the **RUMBLING** of the heavy boulder coming up the pipe tunnel. Then we saw it.

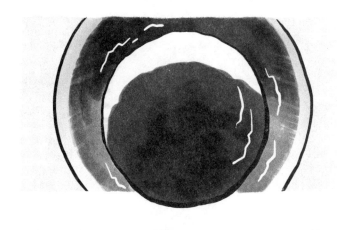

It was **HUGE.** Way bigger than the fake one at Zeke's house. If this boulder hit me the way the pretend one did, I'd be a pancake avatar!

I crawled into the darkness. The tunnel was cold under my hands and knees. I could see the boulder traveling back up the pipe, away from me, so it was just the right time to start crawling.

I raced as fast as I could, desperately feeling the ground for the hole to hide in. The rolling boulder's sound echoed in the distance, getting quieter and quieter. Then suddenly, it began to get louder again.

It was coming back!

I shuffled along, desperate to get to the next hole.

The noise of the boulder in the metal tunnel was **DEAFENING.** Finally, I felt the pipe's floor drop away. I dived into the hole and crouched down in a ball just as the boulder passed over. It sounded like a freight train was running over me.

As soon as it passed, I leaped up to start moving to the next hole. If this was designed like the prototype, then the holes would be getting farther apart.

I shuffled up the pipe as the boulder rolled back down toward the beginning of the tunnel.
I knew it would be turning around soon, so I went into **HYPER-SPEED.**

I plopped down into the next hole, relieved to make it. The boulder rolled over. This time, I waited for it to return. It only had a short way to travel before making the longer journey back to the beginning.

The boulder **THUNDERED** over me again. Once it had passed, I jumped out of the hole and started crawling through the tunnel toward the end. I had to hurry. The light ahead seemed so far away.

The boulder rumbled farther and farther along. But then it started to come back and the rumbling grew **LOUDER.**

Hurry, Ari, I whispered to myself.

I could hear the heavy rock gaining on me. Oof—I was about to get **BLOXXED!**

Hurry!

I could see the light.

The boulder was deafening.

I reached out and launched myself out of the tunnel as I felt the air from the boulder whoosh up my legs. I made it!

"Checkpoint three cleared."

As I stood up, I heard Trip and Jez **CHEERING.**

"Trip, your turn!" I called. "Wait for the boulder to get to you, then when it starts to go back up the tunnel, follow it! That will give you the most time. It'll be faster than you, so crawl **QUICKLY!"**

I waited anxiously, unable to see into the darkness of the tunnel. All I could do was wait for the boulder to reappear at my end each time, and hope that there wasn't a flattened Trip stuck to it.

Finally, I saw a shadow coming toward me. It was Trip.

"GO, TRIP, GO!" I shouted.

The dark, looming shadow of the boulder was gaining on him.

"Faster!" I yelled.

"My energy is running out!" he moaned as he crawled quickly.

The boulder inched closer.

Trip's face came into the light. It was covered in sweat and he

looked **EXHAUSTED.** He
reached out toward me. The
boulder was nipping at his heels.

"I can't!" he cried, extending his arms.

Without thinking, I launched the
top half of my body into the
tunnel and grabbed his hands.
I yanked him as hard as I could.

We both **TUMBLED** out of the mouth of the tunnel with less than a second to spare.

The boulder crashed against the exit of the tunnel and then started rolling away from us.

"Checkpoint three cleared."

"Thanks," Trip huffed, **"BRUH."**

Trip had never called me "bruh" before. Maybe he was changing?

"Five minutes!" Jez screamed.

SATURDAY, FIVE MINUTES TO GO . . .

We climbed the ladder, up and up, to the final platform. My heart sank and I felt like there was a rock as big as the tunnel boulder stuck in the pit of my stomach. It was Jez's obstacle: the **FLAME-AND-LASER JUMPS.** Where was Zeke, the obby pro, when you needed him?!

None of us were able to clear this in the prototype. And neither

could the army avatar in the
demonstration. How were we going
to do this?

"**WAIT!**" I heard Jez scream
from below.

Was someone here? Were we saved?

"I have to tell you the **TRICK**
to this one!" she added.

"There's a trick? Why didn't
you tell us the other day at the
prototype?" I said, confused.

"Zeke's dad said not to reveal it,"

she explained. "He hasn't even told the army avatars. The point is to work it out yourself."

"I don't have time to work it out myself!" I yelled.

"Exactly," said Jez. "So I'm gonna tell you. The secret is **TEAMWORK.**"

"Teamwork? LAME!" Trip cried.

I punched him lightly in the arm. "Dude, listen to her. She **DESIGNED** this thing!"

"The laser can only shoot one at a time. And the fire only shoots one at a time. If you get in a rhythm and **COMMUNICATE,** you should only have to face one of them each at any point."

I looked out to the blocks. Then down to the bubbling lava. Then over to Trip.

"Do you think you can actually listen?" I asked him.

"Listen to you?!" Trip squinted at me, then toward the

BUBBLING LAVA,

and his face softened. "OK," he conceded.

"Ari, jump onto the first block. The fire will come first. Then jump to the second block at the same time as Trip jumps to the first," Jez said. "Ari, you'll need to duck from the laser, and Trip, you'll need to dodge the flame from below. Each time you jump to a new block, do it at the same time and alternate between laser and fire. Got it?"

"Not really," Trip said.

"Well, you have no time!"
Jez yelled. **"FOUR MINUTES!"**

I nodded firmly. "Trip, listen to
my voice," I said. Then I turned
toward the obby.

SATURDAY, FOUR MINUTES TO GO . . .

I leaped onto the first block. I knew
a flame would shoot straight up,
so I dodged to the left.

"Trip, **NOW!**"

I leaped to the second block
just as Trip hit the first block.
As soon as I landed, I knew the
laser would come downward,
so I ducked into a squat. But
I also knew there would be no

flame for me, because the flame
was on Trip.

"Trip, **JUMP!**" I yelled.

I heard Trip jump behind me and
land. This time, I had the flame
and Trip had the laser. I dodged
to the side as the flame shot up.

"Trip, you with me?"

"Yes!"

"Jump, **NOW!**"

We jumped again. I ducked the laser and Trip dodged the flame.

One more jump for me.

"Trip, **NOW!**"

I leaped to the last platform.

"Checkpoint four cleared."

SATURDAY, ONE MINUTE TO GO . . .

"One minute!" Jez warned.

Trip ducked the laser, then got ready for his last jump. Since I was not there to take the fire, I knew he would get one more extra flame.

"I did it!" he yelled, thinking the lasers and fires were done.

"No, LISTEN!" I screamed, getting his attention. **"DODGE NOW!"**

Trip moved just in time as a flame shot upward toward the ceiling. He looked shocked as he took his last leap to the final platform.

"Checkpoint four cleared."

Trip's face was awash with relief. He pulled me into a hug and we fell down on the platform, laughing. I could hear Jez **CHEERING** with delight below.

At that moment, we heard the **WHOOSH** of the metal door and the lights came on. We shielded our eyes, which weren't used to the brightness.

"What on earth is going on in here?!" Zeke's pale-faced dad yelled.

"Dudes, why are you on the obby?" Zeke asked.

"OH, MY BABY!" wailed the mayor.

"Get them down!" the army officials hollered.

As we were lowered to the ground, Zeke and Jez ran up to me and hugged me.

"Wait, did you . . . did you clear the obby?!" Zeke's dad said with wide eyes.

"Sure did," I said with a grin. "But it wasn't me. It was teamwork." I winked at Jez.

"Right, bruh?" I said, extending my arm for a fist bump with Trip.

Trip looked at me, then looked at his mom and everyone standing around. "Don't you call me 'bruh,'" he hissed. "You're the one who **DARED** me to go up there!"

Wait, what?!

Trip turned and hugged his mom, who was giving me death stares.

So much for teamwork. I guess some avatars never change.

SUNDAY MORNING

My computer screen lit up.

> **Zeke:** Bruh, wanna come over this afternoon?

> **Ari:** Sounds cool. Wat you wanna do?

> **Zeke:** Dad is building a new obby and I wanna try it.

> . . .

. . .

. . .

Zeke: JUST KIDDING!

Ari: Too soon, bruh.

Zeke: LOL. Let's go skateboarding.

Ari: I'm in. See you in ten minutes.

Zeke: C u soon!

ALSO AVAILABLE:

AND MORE
ROBLOX
ADVENTURES
COMING SOON!